THE CONFIDENT ME

By Renee C. Clarke

"Confidence happens with practice and action."

-Renee C. Clarke

Hi there! I am Renee, a Pediatric Registered Nurse who moved to the United States from Trinidad and Tobago when I was a child. As a Pediatric Nurse, I take care of kids your age who are usually sick and do not feel so well! Just like you, I enjoyed school and making new friends, but it was not quite easy moving to a new place.

My story is dedicated to each of you! I hope after reading this book, you celebrate who you are, love yourself, and know that you are smart, you are unique, you are beautiful, and you are here on earth for a purpose!

"Mommy, Mommy, I packed all my stuff for our
exciting move to the United States," Kerry-Ann said.
"Great job, Kerry-Ann. I'm so proud of you! We have a long plane ride,
so be sure to get a good night's rest," her mom said.

Kerry-Ann and her mom spent time packing and cleaning for the big move.
Kerry-Ann was eventually exhausted and got ready for bed.
As Kerry-Ann lay in the bed, she thought about how exciting it would be to make
new friends and be in a new place. She was sad to leave all her friends
but very thrilled about seeing her dad again.

"Good morning, Mommy! I am ready for our plane ride.
I cannot wait to see Daddy and meet new friends at school in America,"
said Kerry-Ann.
"I'm so excited! You are going to meet lots of friends! Everyone will love you!
Have you practiced your morning affirmations?" replied her mom.
"Mommy, can you say them with me?" said Kerry-Ann.
"Sure!" her mom said.
"I am smart, I am unique, I am beautiful, and I am here for a purpose!"
they said boldly.

Kerry-Ann and her mom always practiced talking to themselves in the mirror.
It was fun and so easy to do! It reminded them of who they really were before
they faced the big world outside!

Kerry-Ann and her mom took a long plane ride to the United States!
Kerry-Ann stayed awake and witnessed the roads, cars,
and mountains grow smaller and smaller as their plane climbed high in the sky.
She watched the big white clouds and imagined they were shaped
like different animals. She thought about all her friends she had left behind.

"Mommy, I'm a little scared to leave my friends and find new ones,"
Kerry-Ann said.

"Everything will be just fine; I will be right here with you on this journey.
Besides, you are so special, and everyone will love you," replied her mom.

Several hours later, Kerry-Ann and her mom held on to their seats tightly
as the plane finally landed in America!

"That was such a long plane ride! My first time on a plane was spectacular!
I was actually a bit scared about how big the plane was, but I loved it!"
said Kerry-Ann.
"Yes, it was long! You did great!
Thank you for being so amazing," replied her mom.

Kerry-Ann saw her dad from far away, and she ran up to him!

"Daddy, Daddy, it's so great to see you," Kerry-Ann said happily.
"It's so great to see you both. I am so happy we are all here as a family,"
replied her dad.

Kerry-Ann and her family drove around the city
to see all the new places and eventually made it home.

"Mommy, I can't wait for my first day of school
to meet new friends and teachers," Kerry-Ann said.
"Yes, dear! Me too. I am so thrilled about your first day of school.
You are going to do great! Everyone will love you," said her mom.

Kerry-Ann and her mom were so happy about school and eager to meet new friends. Kerry-Ann prepared her clothes for the first day of school. Her mom combed her hair just like she liked it, braids, and curls.

Kerry-Ann entered school with a great spirit and a big smile!
She was a little nervous as she approached other kids,
but she decided to be brave.

"Hello, my name is Kerry-Ann, and I moved to America last week," she said.
"Your name is what? Why do you talk like that, you have a funny accent?
Maryia yelled.

"Talk like what?" Kerry-Ann replied.
"You sound funny and different to us!" Maryia laughed.

"This is how I speak. What's wrong with how I speak?"
Kerry-Ann asked with a confused look.

Maryia and her friends kept laughing and mocking Kerry-Ann.

Kerry-Ann walked away incredibly sad
and decided not to speak to anyone else for the rest of the day.
She could not wait for her mom to arrive to leave school and never go back!

She thought to herself, well, what did I do wrong, and how do I talk?
Everyone where I am from talked like this,
and no one laughed at me there.

Kerry-Ann could not wait to see her mom!
As soon as she spotted her, she ran quickly to the car.

"Kerry-Ann, how was your first day at school? Did you meet new friends?"
her mom asked.
"Mommy, I don't want to go back to school.
Everyone made fun of how I spoke and said I had a funny accent,"
Kerry-Ann said sadly.
"They laughed at how you spoke. You have a beautiful accent!
People all around the world speak differently, that's what makes us all unique!"
her mom said.
They should not laugh at you because your accent is different from theirs,"
her mom quickly replied.
"But what should I do?" Kerry-Ann asked.
"Remember who you are and exactly what I taught you.
Do you remember what that is?" her mom asked.
"Yes, Mommy," Kerry-Ann said. As she wiped her tears, she said,
"I am smart, I am unique, I am beautiful, and I am here for a purpose."
"Yes, you are!" her mom happily replied.

Later that evening, Kerry-Ann and her mom spoke again
about what happened at school.

"Mommy, I am so nervous to go back to school tomorrow.
It really hurt me that those kids made fun of me.
I miss my friends back home," Kerry-Ann said.

"I'm so sorry you feel that way. But just remember:
Sometimes in life, bad things happen to beautiful people,
and you just have to know how strong you are," her mom said.

"Ok, Mommy. Even though I am scared, I will try," Kerry-Ann said with a smile.

Kerry-Ann and her mom discussed all the talents
she was good at and the importance of speaking up for herself.

The next morning, Kerry-Ann and her mom got ready for school.
You could hear Kerry-Ann whispering the affirmations she practiced.

"Kerry-Ann, have a great day at school. Don't forget ..." her mom said.
"Yes, Mommy, do not forget who I am. I am smart, I am unique, I am beautiful,
and I am here for a purpose!" Kerry-Ann said proudly.
"Great job. Yes, you are! I am so proud of you!" replied her mom.

Even though Kerry-Ann was nervous, she decided to be courageous!
She attended her morning classes and then, went to lunch.
Kerry-Ann sat at the lunch table by herself,
hoping not to see Maryia and her friends. As she bit into her apple,
she could see Maryia and her friends walking over to her table. Kerry-Ann's heart
beat fast, but she remembered all that she and her mom talked about.

"There goes the kid with the funny accent," Maryia yelled, laughing.

As all the kids in the group laughed, Kerry-Ann tuned out the noise
and whispered to herself quietly,
"I am smart, I am unique, I am beautiful, and I am brave"

Then Kerry-Ann stood up and said,
"You know, it's not nice to laugh at people. I love my accent, and this is who I am.
I am smart, I am unique, I am beautiful, and I am here for a purpose."

Kerry-Ann grabbed her bags and walked away
feeling confident about her response.
She smiled to herself and was happy she finally spoke up!
Kerry-Ann walked to her next class
and could not wait to tell her mom the story.

Later that afternoon, Maryia and Kerry-Ann attended the same class. Maryia was alone this time and did not have all her friends with her. As they sat in class, Kerry-Ann could see Maryia looking at her on occasion.

At the end of class, Maryia walked up to Kerry-Ann and said,
"You know, I am sorry I laughed at you.
I thought it was cool that you were different,
but I did not know how to say it."
Kerry-Ann smiled and said, "I forgive you."
"So, can we start over? My name is Maryia, and welcome to our school.
So where did you say you were from again?"
"Thank you. Nice to meet you! I am from Trinidad and Tobago,
a small island in the Caribbean," Kerry-Ann said.

Kerry-Ann and Maryia spent some time talking after class and realized they had lots of similarities. They both loved running, dancing, and playing at the park.

As the school bell rang for dismissal, Kerry-Ann ran outside to meet her mom.

"So, Kerry-Ann, how was school today?" her mom asked.
"Mommy, school was great! Maryia and her friends laughed at me again,
but this time I remembered what you said: I must be strong!
I told them that it is not nice to laugh at people and who I am...
smart, unique, and beautiful," Kerry-Ann proudly said.

"Kerry-Ann, I am so proud of you! You are so brave and strong!
You did amazing at standing up for yourself," her mom said.

Kerry-Ann and her mom spent the car ride home
talking about her experience at school.
Kerry-Ann realized that despite her differences,
confidently reminding herself of her uniqueness was important.
In addition, Maryia learned that even though other people may be different,
it is important to respect others and accept them.

DISCUSSION BONUS!

Spend some time talking about the story and how it can be applied to you!

What is Confidence?

In the story, Kerry-Ann was first scared to stand up for herself, but her mom built up her confidence. Here discuss what confidence is and what it is NOT!

CONFIDENCE:

Confidence is believing in yourself and your talents.

Confidence is knowing what you are good at and accepting it.

Confidence is feeling great about yourself and your abilities.

Confidence is built from the inside.

Confidence is listening and learning.

Confidence keeps trying and does not give up!

CONFIDENCE IS NOT:

Confidence is NOT comparing yourself to others.

Confidence is NOT only what you look like.

Confidence is NOT being perfect.

Confidence is NOT knowing everything.

"Blessed are those who trust and place their Confidence in God" – Jeremiah 17:7

Thank you for reading!
Please leave a review on Amazon;
I would love to hear your feedback!
For coloring pages of scenes from this book, visit
@confidentwithpurpose
on instagram and download free material!

Affirmations are a great way to remind yourself of who you are and all the strengths you have!

Sample "I am" affirmations:

I am enough. I am unique.
I am loved. I am beautiful.
I am smart.
I am born for a purpose.
I am a masterpiece and a work in progress.
My gifts and talents are important.

Make your own "I am" affirmations:

....

....

....

....

....

Let's talk about your uniqueness!
Write down the answers:

What makes you special?

....

....

What are you great at?

....

....

What do you do if a classmate or anyone makes fun of you?

....

....

What do you do if a classmate dislikes the following?
a. Hair   b. Clothes   c. Shoes   d. Accent   e. You

....

....

....

....